Dear Parents and Educators,

Welcome to Penguin Young Readers! As parents and educators, you know that each child develops at his or her own pace—in terms of speech, critical thinking, and, of course, reading. Penguin Young Readers recognizes this fact. As a result, each Penguin Young Readers book is assigned a traditional easy-to-read level (1–4) as well as a Guided Reading Level (A–P). Both of these systems will help you choose the right book for your child. Please refer to the back of each book for specific leveling information. Penguin Young Readers features esteemed authors and illustrators, stories about favorite characters, fascinating nonfiction, and more!

Dick and Jane: Go Away, Spot

LEVEL 2

GUIDED READING LEVEL **E**

This book is perfect for a **Progressing Reader** who:
- can figure out unknown words by using picture and context clues;
- can recognize beginning, middle, and ending sounds;
- can make and confirm predictions about what will happen in the text; and
- can distinguish between fiction and nonfiction.

Here are some **activities** you can do during and after reading this book:
- Use the Pictures: Many times when a child reads a book, the pictures can tell the child something else about the story. Use the pictures to answer the following questions:
  - On page 8, what is the "something" that Dick sees?
  - On page 10, how does Puff help?
  - On pages 12 and 13, what is Puff playing with?
  - On page 23, why does Dick say, "Go away, Spot"?
  - On pages 27 and 28, what is the funny "something" that Jane, Dick, and Sally see?

Remember, sharing the love of reading with a child is the best gift you can give!

—Bonnie Bader, EdM
  Penguin Young Readers program

*Penguin Young Readers are leveled by independent reviewers applying the standards developed by Irene Fountas and Gay Su Pinnell in *Matching Books to Readers: Using Leveled Books in Guided Reading*, Heinemann, 1999.

Penguin Young Readers
Published by the Penguin Group
Penguin Group (USA) Inc., 375 Hudson Street, New York, New York 10014, USA
Penguin Group (Canada), 90 Eglinton Avenue East, Suite 700, Toronto, Ontario M4P 2Y3, Canada
(a division of Pearson Penguin Canada Inc.)
Penguin Books Ltd., 80 Strand, London WC2R 0RL, England
Penguin Group Ireland, 25 St. Stephen's Green, Dublin 2, Ireland (a division of Penguin Books Ltd.)
Penguin Group (Australia), 250 Camberwell Road, Camberwell, Victoria 3124, Australia
(a division of Pearson Australia Group Pty. Ltd.)
Penguin Books India Pvt. Ltd., 11 Community Centre, Panchsheel Park, New Delhi—110 017, India
Penguin Group (NZ), 67 Apollo Drive, Rosedale, Auckland 0632, New Zealand
(a division of Pearson New Zealand Ltd.)
Penguin Books (South Africa) (Pty.) Ltd., 24 Sturdee Avenue,
Rosebank, Johannesburg 2196, South Africa

Penguin Books Ltd., Registered Offices: 80 Strand, London WC2R 0RL, England

Dick and Jane is a registered trademark of Addison-Wesley Educational Publishers, Inc.
From GUESS WHO. Copyright © 1951 by Scott Foresman and Company, copyright renewed 1979.
From THE NEW WE WORK AND PLAY. Copyright © 1956 by Scott Foresman and Company,
copyright renewed 1984. All rights reserved. First published in 2003 by Grosset & Dunlap, an imprint
of Penguin Group (USA) Inc. Published in 2012 by Penguin Young Readers, an imprint of
Penguin Group (USA) Inc., 345 Hudson Street, New York, New York 10014. Manufactured in China.

Library of Congress Control Number: 2003016958

ISBN 978-0-448-43404-9   10 9 8 7 6 5 4 3 2 1

ALWAYS LEARNING

PEARSON

Dick and Jane
Go Away, Spot

Penguin Young Readers
An Imprint of Penguin Group (USA) Inc.

Contents

Chapter 1
Jane and Puff

Oh, Jane.

I see something.

Look, Jane, look.

Look here.

8

Come, Puff.

Come here.

Jump, little Puff.

Jump, jump.

Look, Baby Sally.

Come here and look.

See Puff.

Puff can help.

Puff can help Jane.

Chapter 2
See Puff Go

Come here, Dick.

Come and see Puff.

See Puff play.

See Puff jump.

Puff can jump and play.

Oh, Mother, Mother.

Come and look.

See Puff jump and play.

See little Puff play.

Look, Mother, look.

See Puff jump and play.

Oh, oh, oh.

See Puff jump down.

See Puff jump and go.

Jump down, funny Puff.

Jump down.

Jump down.

Go, go, go.

Chapter 3
Tim and Sally Help

Sally said, "Look, Mother.

I can help.

See Baby Sally help.

See little Tim help.

See little Tim go.

Oh, see little Tim go."

Sally said, "Look, Tim.

Look down here.

I see cookies.

I see cookies down here.

Cookies, cookies, cookies."

Sally said, "Come, Mother.

We can go.

Look here, Mother.

Cookies, cookies, cookies.

Come, Mother, come.

We can go."

Chapter 4
Go Away, Spot

Dick said, "Down, Spot.

I cannot play.

Down, Spot, down.

Go away, little Spot.

Go away and play."

Sally said, "Oh, Spot.

We see you.

Tim and I see you.

And little Puff sees you.

We see you, funny Spot."

Dick said, "Oh, oh, oh.

Go away, Spot.

You cannot help.

You cannot play here."

Sally said, "Run away, Spot.

Run, run, run."

Chapter 5
Puff, Tim, and Spot

Sally said, "See Puff go.

Puff can jump down.

Puff can run away.

See little Tim.

Tim cannot jump down.

Tim cannot run away."

Dick said, "Come, Spot.

You and I can play.

Look here, Spot.

Cookies, cookies.

Jump, Spot, jump."

26

Dick said, "See Spot.

Oh, see Spot jump."

Jane said, "Mother, Mother.

We see something funny."

"Come here.

Come here.

Come and see Spot."

Chapter 6
Spot Helps Sally

Look, Spot, look.

Find Dick and Jane.

Go, Spot, go.

Help Sally find Dick.

Help Sally find Jane.

Go, Spot.

Go and find Dick.

Go and find Jane.

Run, Spot, run.

Run and find Dick.

Run and find Jane.

Oh, oh, oh.

Spot can find Dick.

Spot can find Jane.

Oh, oh.

Spot can help Sally.

Spot can play.